Roxanna
& the Quest for the Time-Bird

Script: Letendre
Art: Loisel

NANTIER·BEALL·MINOUSTCHINE
Publishing co.
new york

Letendre and Loisel as seen by Loisel

©Dargaud Editeur 1983 de Loisel et Letendre
©NBM 1987 for English translation
ISBN 0-918348-30-7

Write for a complete catalog:
NBM
156 E. 39th St.
New York, NY 10016

Dep. Legal: B-44067/86 ALOGRAN

Printed in Spain by NORMA Serveis Gràfics
Tx 50293 - Fax (343) 2323654 ☎ 245 64 03/232 62 12

SOMEWHERE, LOST IN THE MARSH OF *THE WALK OF THE VEILS OF FROTH*...

NOW, *ANYTHING* CAN HAPPEN, MY LITTLE MASTER!

TODAY'S THE DAY I COME OUT OF MY DEN AND THROW MYSELF INTO ADVENTURE...

ARE YOU LISTENING, MY LITTLE *FURRY*?

WITCH-PRINCESS MARA, MY MOTHER, HAS FINALLY DECIDED.

SHE GAVE ME A MESSAGE TO BRING OVER TO THE LEGENDARY KNIGHT *BRAGON*.

DRÜ...

WHO, IF HE'S STILL WHAT HE USED TO BE, WILL COME RUNNING. THEN WILL START ONE OF THE MOST DANGEROUS UNDERTAKINGS EVER SEEN ON *AKBAR*...

IT WILL BE...

DRÜ DRÜ

THE QUEST FOR THE TIME BIRD!

7

8

9

SLOWLY, AS THE NIGHT DESCENDED UPON AKBAR'S SKY SO DID ANGER FILL AND CHOKE BRAGON!

HE HAD JUST BEEN TREATED AS NEVER BEFORE!

BY THE FANGS OF THE BORAK! MARA IS MAKING FUN OF ME!

AFTER ALL THESE YEARS OF SILENCE AND NEGLECT, NOW SHE SENDS HER...BITCH TO PROVOKE ME!...IN MY HOME! IN MY VERY DOMAIN!

BITCH!

ME?! A BITCH!

DRÜ!

BRAGON, I WILL NOT LET YOU...

DRÜ! DRÜ!

AH, SHUT UP! YOU AND YOUR CRITTER!

EASY, MY LITTLE MASTER, EASY...

DRÜ!

HE'S A FURRY... MARA SAYS HE HAS STRANGE POWERS!

BAH! POWERS, MAGIC, SORCERY! RIGHT! I RECOGNIZE WELL THERE ALL OF MARA'S ARTIFICES.

BUT...I AM NO LONGER A YOUNG KNIGHT...

DRU...

...TO BE WON OVER AND THEN DITCHED AFTER THE FIRST QUARREL.

I AM STILL BRAGON... THE KNIGHT...

YEAH... WELL... I WAS...

'CAUSE NOW... YOU KNOW...

NOW IT'S ONLY UP TO YOU TO BECOME THAT AGAIN...

?

LOOK! MARA GAVE ME THIS MESSAGE. IT WILL EXPLAIN ALL!!

ALL!

HUM?...

STIK!

MARA!

13

HIS FELONY WAS REVEALED AND FAILED!!

WITH THE HELP OF THEIR BOOK OF MAGIC, THE GODS LET LOOSE A HORRIBLE ENCHANTMENT!

THE MAGIC FORCES CONFRONTED EACH OTHER IN A DEMONIC BATTLE!

FINALLY, RAMOR WAS PARALYZED, VANQUISHED BY THE ENCHANTMENT!

INSANE WITH RAGE, HE WAS SUCKED INTO THE HEART OF A CONCH, HIS PRISON!

LONG AFTER, THE GODS, OLD AND BATTLE-WEARY, RETIRED INTO A SECRET WORLD...

BUT LO! RAMOR, FORGOTTEN WITHIN THE MEANDERS OF THE CONCH, REMAINED!

HIS HATRED GREW AS HE AWAITED THE HOUR OF HIS DELIVERANCE!

THIS HOUR HAS COME NEAR... DESTRUCTION AND DEATH WILL THEN TAKE AKBAR OVER!

THE ENCHANTMENT WHICH HAS KEPT RAMOR WILL VANISH THE NIGHT OF THE CHANGING SEASON!

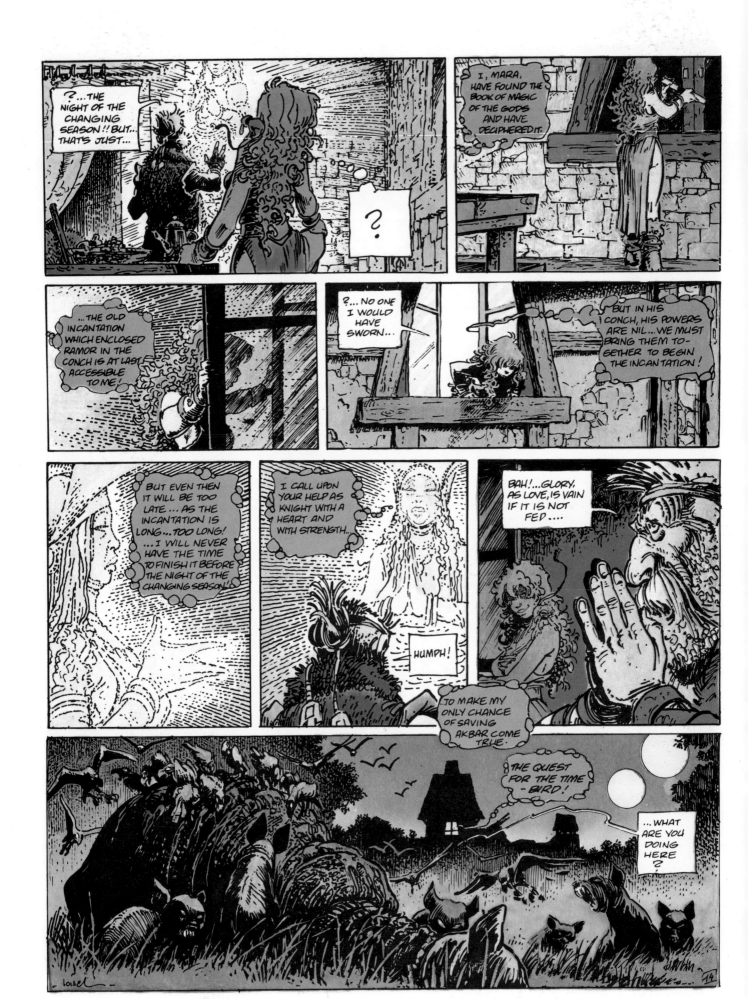

LATER, AT THE FAR END OF THE HIGH PLAINS OF THE MEDIR.

TAKE CARE! WE'RE ENTERING THE LAND OF THE SEVEN STEPS!

BRAGON KNEW THIS WAY WELL! THE FIRST STEP WAS THE KINGDOM OF THE GREY GRELONS, ...ITS WITCH-PRINCE WAS SHAN-THUNG...

...AND IT'S NAME WAS...

THE WALK OF THE GAPING LANDS!

HE ALSO KNEW THERE WAS NO TIME TO LOSE.

BRAGON! THE LOPWINDS HAVE HAD IT!

THERE! AN ABODE: THE SACRED CAVE OF THE GREY GRELONS!

THERE WERE ONLY NINE DAYS REMAINING TIL THE NIGHT OF THE CHANGING SEASONS!

NOT ONE MORE!

19

O.K., FINE... DON'T GET ANGRY!... WHERE ARE WE?

I'M NOT ANGRY!

WE ARE IN THE SACRED CAVE, THE SANCTUARY OF THE GREY GRELONS...THEY COME HERE TO DIE...

WHY HERE?

BECAUSE FOR REBIRTH THEY NEED A SOURCE ...AND HERE IT IS! THE SOURCE OF THE RIVER DOL!

HEE-HEE!

MEANWHILE, AT THE FOOT OF THE MOUNTAIN!

2 STRANGERS ARE DESACRATING OUR CAVE!

?!

WE MUST KILL THEM ZA-RHIM!

THEIR PRESENCE IS SACRILEGE!

ENOUGH!

IS ONE OF THEM A MAN...A BEARDED KNIGHT?

AND IF SO...THEN... SHAN-THUNG PREDICTED IT!

LAUGHTER?

HEE...HEE...HEE...

YES, I HEARD IT ALSO...IT WAS RUNNING SOMEWHERE OVER THERE.

AGAIN! OVER THERE! LISTEN!!

HEE

HEE

?

21

23

24

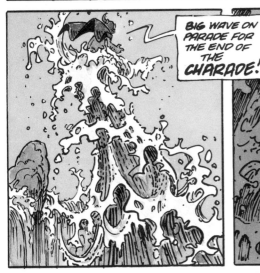

26

SOON AFTER, ONCE ROXANNA AND BRAGON HAD RECOVERED...

NOW THAT'S BETTER, BRAVE AND WISE! THIS TRICK WAS ONLY TO OPEN YOUR EYES!

BUT WHO, TELL ME... WHO... OF THE MODEL OR THE MIRROR REFLECTS BETTER?

SPLICH!

HOOHEE, HOO-HEE!

HEE, HEE!

PLOUF!

SPLICH!

SPLICH!

STRANGE CHARACTER!

STRANGE YES...

...AND DANGEROUS!

WELL, IF HIS HONEST CRAZY-INESS CHOSE AN HONEST CAMP, MARA COULD HAVE...

...A PRECIOUS ALLY. YESSIR! THAT DE-MON WOULD RAISE A FLAG UPSIDE DOWN!

ANYWAY! AS LONG AS YOU HAVE THE RIGHT ANSWERS FOR HIM, WE'LL BE OK...

LET'S GO... MARA IS WAITING!

?!

I SALUTE YOU, NOBLE KNIGHT BRAGON! WE WERE NOT EXPECTING YOU SO SOON... SHAN-TUNG, OUR PRINCE, WILL BE HAPPY TO GREET YOU IN HIS CITY OF IR-WEIG!

BRAGON ?...

PATIENCE, ROXANNA...

TO REFUSE AN INVI-TATION FROM SHAN-TUNG IS SUICIDE...

...AND DON'T FORGET, HE HAS THE CONCH!

28

IT WAS TIME TO GO... THE GREY-GRELONS WERE WAITING ONLY FOR ROXANNA AND BRAGON...

OK, WE'RE READY!

HOLD ON, BRAGON, THERE'S STILL SOMETHING WE MUST DO...

OH, YES... TRUE...

THE LOPWINDS, HUH?...

YES, BRAGON, THE LOPWINDS...

? WHAT ARE YOU TALKING ABOUT?

HUMM...WHEN WE CAME INTO THEIR SACRED CAVE, WE DESECRATED IT... WELL IT'S OBVIOUS, ROXANNA...WE MUST MAKE AMENDS!

? AMENDS?... YOU MEAN... A SACRIFICE!

EXACTLY!

I SEE THAT YOU ARE READY TO ACCEPT OUR CUSTOMS, BRAGON... AND THAT THE DAYS WHERE YOU WOULD HAVE ANSWERED ME WITH YOUR AXE ARE GONE... HOW WISE!

THUNDER! HE'S MAKING FUN OF ME...

ALRIGHT, ENOUGH OF THIS FUSS... GET ON WITH IT!

LOK-THAR! TAKE CARE OF THE OFFERINGS!

HEY! ENOUGH OF THAT!

HEE! HEE!

GET BACK! AREN'T THE LOPWINDS ENOUGH?

?

ZA-RHIM! TELL YOUR PEOPLE TO STOP, OR ELSE!

HOLD IT!

IT WAS TO BE EXPECTED! THIS IS THE SEASON OF LOWLY DISCOMFORTS!

BLOOD AND THUNDER THE SEASON OF LOWLY DISCOMFORTS!

THE WORST!

29

IMMEDIATELY, BRAGON RUSHED FORWARD...

LET HER BE, SCUM!

NO TIME TO EXPLAIN, ROXANNA, PUT THIS ON...

YOU'RE EXCITING THEM!

?... ME? EXCITING THEM?

BUT... HOW?

ONE WONDERS.

SOON AFTER...

IT'S DONE, ZA-RHIM... THE DESECRATION IS ERASED.

GOOD! LET'S GET GOING!

ALL DAY, THE LITTLE GROUP HAD FOLLOWED THE WAY OF THE RIVER IN SILENCE.

...THEY HAD GOTTEN DEEP INTO THE WALK OF GAPING LANDS...

FINALLY, CLOSE TO IR-WEIG...

?

GO ON WITHOUT ME. I WILL CHECK THIS OUT.

?...BRAGON, LOOK!

!?

LLIR WARRIORS! ONE OF THEM IS HEADING OUR WAY!

NO... DO NOT ATTEMPT ANYTHING... HE IS AT SHAN-TUNG'S SERVICE!

WHAT?

OUR PEOPLE ARE WEAK, BRAGON...

?!

LLIR WARRIORS WERE REPUTED TO BE THE MOST FEARSOME MERCENARIES EVER SEEN ON AKBAR.

AND THEIR CHIEF COULD ONLY BE THE WORST OF THEM ALL.

...AND WAR IS NEAR!

THIS CAN'T BE!!

28

30

SUDDENLY...

MAY MOTHER-LIGHTNING BREAK YOU APART!

SHÖÖF!!

CURSED FOOLS! HOW DARE YOU BREAK THE SACRED RULES OF HOSPITALITY OF IR-WEIG!

BE GONE! BE GONE!

HOLY FURY! ROXANNA ARE YOU ALRIGHT?

YEAH... BUT WHO'S THE LUNATIC WHO...

OOOH... MY HEAD...

SHAN-TUNG!

OH, THERE HE IS. 'ABOUT TIME! MY PATIENCE IS RUNNING OUT!

DRÜ...

HOLD ME, BULROG... THIS MAGIC DRAINS ME.

I AM HERE PRINCE.

A FEW MOMENTS LATER.

WHAT GOOD FORTUNE TO SEE YOU AGAIN, PRINCE... YOUR INTERVENTIONS ARE ALWAYS SO... STRIKING!

WE ARE LIVING DIFFICULT DAYS, BRAGON...

WELL, I GUESS I'D BETTER GET DRESSED!

THE LAND OF THE 7 WALKS IS ON THE VERGE OF WAR... AND THE SEASON OF LOWLY DISCOMFORTS HAS CLOISTERED OUR WOMEN AND KEEPS US AWAY FROM THEIR...

CHARMS!

LET'S BE HONEST, BRAGON ...YOUR WELL-ENDOWED FOLLOWER DOESN'T BELONG HERE!

ROXANNA IS NOT MY FOLLOWER!

HEH, HEH... I'LL BET... LIKE 'EM YOUNG AND TENDER, EH?

BULROG!

THE PRISONER HAS DISAPPEARED!!

33

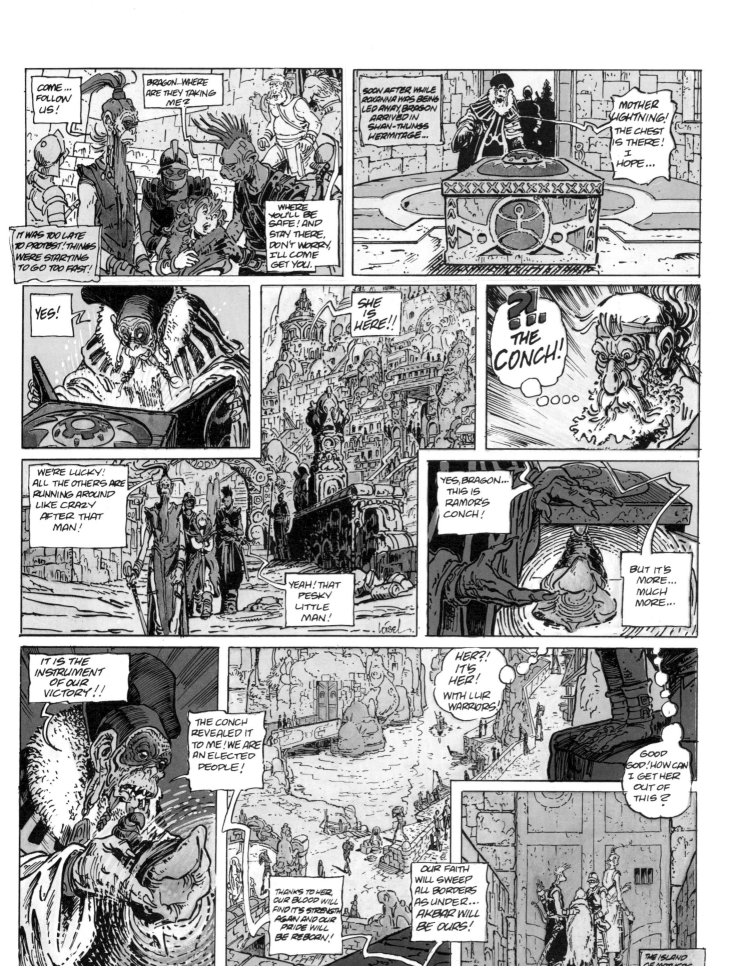

WHO WAS THE MYSTERIOUS LLIR WARRIOR WHO FREED ROXANNA?... WHAT WERE HIS INTENTIONS?

NO TIME TO EXPLAIN... I'M HERE TO ...HUH... PROTECT YOU!

TO PROTECT ME?... AGAINST WHAT?

DAMN!

QUICK! GET DOWN!

HEY! WHAT'S THE MATTER?

THERE'S A... LLIR WARRIOR COMING!

INDEED, THE MESSENGER SENT BY BULROG WAS RUSHING TOWARD THE ISLAND!

SOON.

OPEN THE DOORS! QUICK, BULROG'S ORDERS! I'M COMING TO FETCH THE FOREIGNER!

? AGAIN?

YOU GUYS BETTER MAKE UP YOUR MINDS... WE JUST GAVE HER TO ONE OF YOUR GUYS SENT BY SHAN-THUNG!

BY SHAN-THUNG!... BUT...THAT'S IMPOSSIBLE...!

BULROG WILL BE FURIOUS... THE BEARDED MAN SEEMS TO HAVE PUT HIM IN A RAGE!

THAT'S YOUR BUSINESS!

DID YOU HEAR THAT? BRAGON'S IN DANGER. WE MUST HELP HIM!

OH HE'S FAMOUS FOR GETTING OUT OF THIS KIND OF TROUBLE BY HIMSELF!

NO WAY! I'M GOING!

HEY, WAIT! IT COULD BE DANGEROUS!

YOU BETTER BELIEVE IT!

HOLY CRIPES! TO SAY I ALMOST HAD HER!

HEY WAIT FOR ME!

42

BE DAMNED! YOU WANT A VICTIM? ...FINE...

DRÜ!

HERE I AM!

BY THE FANGS OF BORAK! THIS GIRL IS GIVING ME THE BEST LESSON IN COURAGE I'VE EVER SEEN!

? WHERE IS SHE? I CAN'T SEE.

A HEAVY SILENCE FELL ON THE CROWD.

HANG ON, FURRY, MY PLAN IS WORKING!

LET'S WASTE NO TIME, KIDDO... WE'VE GOT TO GET OUT OF HERE NOW!

SHE KNOWS WHAT SHE IS DOING... IT'S OUR TURN!

YEAH, SURE... BUT WHAT ABOUT ROXANNA?

THEN: PANDEMONIUM! THE GREY-GRELONS RUSHED IN HER DIRECTION!

WE'RE OFF!

RAAH! THOSE TITS!

I WANT HER!

SHE'S MINE!

NO! BULROG WANTS HIM ALIVE!

HELLO, ROXANNA!

45

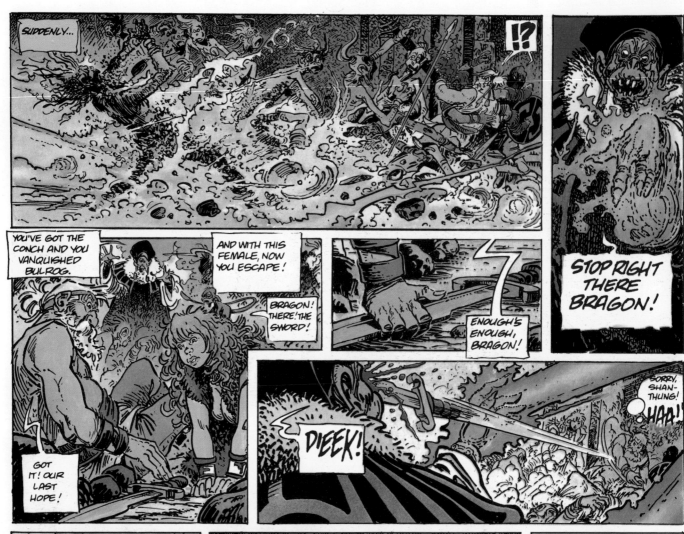

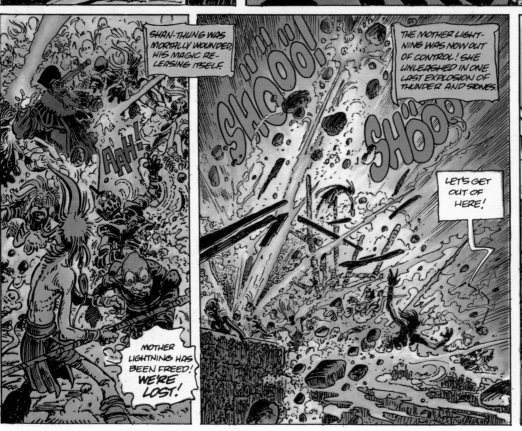

AND SOON AFTER, TAKING ADVANTAGE OF THE PANIC SPREADING IN IR-WEIG, A SMALL BOAT WAS SAILING AWAY...

ON BOARD, A TRIO OF HEROES...

SHE LEFT BEHIND HER...

...A CITY IN RUINS...

...A DEAD PRINCE-SORCERER...

...AND A LLIR WARRIOR CRAVING VENGEANCE.

I'LL GET YOU, BRAGON!

ON THE RIVER DOL, RAMOR'S CONCH WAS SLOWLY MAKING ITS WAY BACK TO MARA'S WALK...

AND SO FINISHED THE FIRST LEG IN THE QUEST FOR THE TIME-BIRD.

SCRIPT: LETENDRE
ART: LOISEL
COLOR: YVES LENCOT

THE END